ARNOLD DOBRIN

"On his first day in Rome, Henry James wrote in his journal: 'Now, for the first time, I live.' I wish I too could have felt such a sudden poetic revelation but the truth was far different. I was confused by the narrow streets and *piazzas*, distracted by the noise, made ill by the cooking and maddened by the traffic. On my second trip I explored the city more thoroughly, felt comfortable and stopped complaining. Three years later I went to Rome to live and then, very suddenly, the miracle happened. The layers of history were no longer simply 'significant historical sites' but an integral part of the life around me. I saw that the famous urbane indifference of the Romans is no thicker than a slice of Italian veal. I grew to love the fragrance of the café espresso drifting through the streets in the late afternoon; I wanted my coffee blacker and stronger. And when I began to understand the attitude of the Romans toward their children I realized that now, for the first time, I was really beginning to live...."

Arnold Dobrin was born in Omaha, Nebraska, brought up in Los Angeles and now lives in Westport, Conn., with his wife and two children.

Carmello was walking home with his grandfather Nonno—the beloved Nonno who worked the Pulcinella puppets in the park. "Someday," Nonno had promised, "Carmello, I will show you how to work the puppets!" But whenever Carmello begged, "When, Nonno?" the old man's answer was always the same. "*Pazienza!* You must have *pazienza*." Someday seemed a long time away. Now as they turned down the Via della Scala, they saw the fat tabby cat and Nonno commented, "Soon we will be calling her Mama."

That day came quickly! On a chilly morning—near Christmastime—Carmello found the tabby and her newborn kittens. The tabby was a street cat—she belonged to no one. If the tiny kittens were left outside in the cold, Carmello was sure they would die.

But when he begged his mother to let him bring the cats home, her answer was firm. "Never will a cat come into our apartment while I am Mama here!"

A charming and engrossing Christmas tale. It takes place in Rome, but it could happen to any boy anywhere.

CARMELLO'S CAT

The Story of a Roman Christmas

Carmello was walking home with his grandfather Nonno—the beloved Nonno who worked the Pulcinella puppets in the park. "Someday," Nonno had promised "Carmello, I will show you how to work the puppets!" But whenever Carmello begged, "When, Nonno?" the old man's answer was always the same. "Pazienza! You must have pazienza." Someday seemed a long time away. Now as they turned down the Via della Scala, they saw the fat tabby cat and Nonno commented, "Soon we will be calling her Mamma." That day came quickly! On a chilly morning— near Christmastime—Carmello found the tabby and her new-born kittens. The tabby was a street cat—she belonged to no one. If the tiny kittens were left outside in the cold, Carmello was sure they would die. But when he begged his mother to let him bring the cats home, her answer was firm. "Never will a cat come into our apartment while I am Mamma here!" How Carmello solves this problem makes a charming and engrossing Christmas tale. It takes place in Rome, but it could happen to any boy anywhere.

CARMELLO'S CAT

The Story of a Roman Christmas

BY

ARNOLD DOBRIN

Coward McCann Inc. • New York

BOOKS BY ARNOLD DOBRIN

Picture Books

TARO AND THE SEA TURTLES
A Tale of Japan

LITTLE MONK AND THE TIGER
A Tale of Thailand

CARMELLO'S CAT
The Story of a Roman Christmas

Biography

AARON COPLAND
His Life and Times

CARMELLO'S CAT

Christmas was coming. Carmello could smell it in the air—a wonderful smell of freshly made candy, nougat and fudge, roasted nuts and sandwiches of hot pork flavored with rosemary. All the delicious fragrances floated on the cold December air up to Carmello's apartment, just around the corner from the Piazza Navona.

By stretching his neck a little, he could get a good view of the big square, which was now bustling with confusion and noise as men put up the hundreds of little stalls where toys and Christmas decorations would soon be sold.

For weeks Carmello had been reminding his mother and father of the present that he wanted for Christmas. He was not the kind of boy who wanted a lot of toys but those he wanted, he wanted very much. And what he wanted were puppets, real puppets—and a stage. A big stage.

More than once his father had had to say, "Enough Carmello! Your mother and I understand exactly what you want for Christmas. Maybe we can get it for you, maybe not. But now paziènza, paziènza. You must have patience."

That is, except when his mother wanted him to do something. Now she was calling to him, and he could tell that she wouldn't have much patience if he lingered on the balcony. Quickly he went into the kitchen, where she was filling a big thermos bottle with hot soup.

"Here," she said as she wrapped it carefully in a paper bag. "Your grandfather was coughing badly when he went to the park this morning. He never should have gone at all. Take this to him—it will keep him warm until lunch. And while you are going, take this—food for the cats."

Carmello went down the steps two at a time. The hall was dark and damp but already filled with the smell of the cooking tomato sauces that the women were preparing for lunch. In a

moment, he was in the bright, cold December sunshine. As soon as he turned the corner he saw them—the neighborhood cats. They had been there as long as he could remember, living in the courtyards and gardens behind the high walls—wherever they could find a sheltered spot. They belonged to no one special but were always there—prowling around, looking for food and not getting too close to anyone—unless he happened to have something to eat.

Once or twice a day an old man or woman—sometimes a child—would come to feed them. Carmello often came. He liked to see the way the cats suddenly darted from behind walls and down from rooftops, until all at once there was a swarm of them scrambling around his feet for food.

Whatever he brought they liked—for it seemed that long ago the Roman cats had learned not to be too particular about their food. Scraps of meat or fish were favorites, but leftover macaroni or spaghetti disappeared just as quickly.

Carmello talked to the cats softly, just as he saw older people talk to them. He never coddled or pampered them but spoke just the way you might speak to another person. And the cats seemed to treat him with equal, if distant, respect.

How hungry they all were today! Carmello watched the big gray one that always took more than his share, the thin, sick-looking white cat that could never get enough and the little black kitten with the lame leg. And there was Carmello's favorite—the striped tabby. She was getting so fat. Carmello smiled to himself as he watched her waddling around the food like a silly fat duck.

Carmello wanted to stay and watch the cats finish their meal but he thought of his grandfather working in the park, and he remembered how cold he would be by now. He walked fast, hurrying through the narrow, busy streets—so narrow that he could almost touch the people at work in their little shops on either side. He had known all of them since he was a baby.

"Buon giorno, Carmello," the shoemaker called.

"Buon giorno," said the butcher, smiling.

"Buon giorno," the grocer said.

Carmello answered "Good morning" cheerfully to all of them—these busy men bundled up in heavy dark sweaters, their faces red and shiny from the cold. Most of them would stay in this little street all of their lives, selling vegetables or meat or mending shoes. It could be a good life, Carmello supposed, but it was not for him. Nonno, his grandfather, had taught him about a different kind of life—full of fun and magic and excitement.

There was Nonno now—or rather, there was the tiny stage behind which his grandfather worked—the Pulcinella puppet stage—surrounded by a small group of children who were giggling and screaming with delight. The show was just ending. Suddenly the little curtains were pulled together, and a few seconds later Nonno came out of the door in the back of the stage.

As Carmello watched his grandfather drink his hot soup from the thermos he asked, "Why are there so few children in the park today?"

"They are in the Piazza Navona, waiting for the toy stalls to open." Nonno smiled his mischievous old smile and his eyes twinkled. "Most children do not know what they want. They are not like Carmello, who has only one idea in his head!"

Carmello knew Nonno was remembering all the times when he had begged his grandfather, "Please, Nonno, let me work the puppets. Let me go behind the stage."

"Not now, Carmello—when you are older."

"Please, Nonno."

"No, Carmello—you must have paziènza, paziènza. You are still a little boy. But the time will come—sooner than you think."

Always the same answer—paziènza!

Carmello was surprised when Nonno started to lock up the stage and put it away under the trees. "But it is still early. Why are you leaving now?" he asked.

Nonno coughed and pulled his scarf tighter around his neck. "Because it is cold and I am tired. Because Christmas is coming and the children are much too excited to watch puppets in the park." Taking Carmello's hand, he said as they walked away, "Every winter I think, 'This will be my last winter to work in the park.' And then when spring comes, I think, 'If only I can stay just one year more.'"

Together they walked through the park and into the cold, sunny streets crowded with Christmas shoppers. Near the Piazza Navona, Carmello smelled a familiar sweet fragrance. He breathed in deeply and knew what it was—the same rich smell of Christmas—fresh candy and roasted chestnuts. He couldn't help walking a little faster.

When they turned the corner into the Piazza, Carmello saw that the men had almost finished putting up the toy stalls. Everywhere the merchants were busy unpacking toys and setting them out—big beautiful dolls in fresh, crisp dresses, shiny silver space suits and walkie-talkies, electric trains and countless boxes full of wonderful toys. Other stalls were bright with boxes of Christmas ornaments, and in still others, women were stirring the big black pots of hot, bubbling candy.

Carmello tugged at Nonno's hand. He pointed at the puppets that he had seen last year. There were six of them, each carefully carved out of wood, with fine funny noses and life-like hands. They wore bright new clothes and behind them was the stage that Carmello wanted too—the big stage with real red velvet curtains. Soon they would all be his.

"Mama and Papa are going to buy these for me for Christmas," he told Nonno.

Nonno squeezed Carmello's hand a little tighter. "Don't count on it," he said. "They are very expensive."

But Carmello did not want to think about that. He imagined himself behind the stage, working the puppets while a great crowd of small children giggled and laughed with delight.

They walked through big groups of children admiring the toys and

turned down the Via della Scala, where Carmello's family lived.

The bright sun of the morning had disappeared behind heavy gray clouds and every once in a while Carmello could feel a great drop of cold rain fall on his nose. He pushed his hands deeper in his pockets and felt sorry for the cats that now huddled together under the dripping trees. Even after the big breakfast Carmello had given them they looked thin and hungry—all except the tabby. "Look, Nonno," Carmello said, pointing to her. "Have you ever seen such a fat cat?"

Nonno stopped walking and looked at the tabby thoughtfully. Then he smiled and said, "She is fat now, Carmello, but soon she will be thin again. Then we will be calling her 'Mamma.'"

So the tabby was carrying kittens!

Of course—why hadn't Carmello realized it before, when he saw her waddling like a duck? From now on he must make sure that she got first chance at the food he brought. And he would have to bring a little more than he usually did because in the winter—suddenly he remembered a day last winter when he had gone to feed the cats. In the wet leaves had been two dead pink kittens.

Carmello wanted to make sure that wouldn't happen this time.

After lunch Carmello's family went to their rooms to rest for a while. Carmello's room was cold, and he snuggled deep under his blankets to try to get warm.

Out of the corner of his eye he looked at all his treasures scattered around the room. In the gray light of the afternoon the only thing that shone was the bright metal armor of the Sicilian marionette that he had been given last Christmas. But that was the only one worth saving. All the others looked terribly old and worn, their bodies broken, fingers lost, their clothes torn and faded. He was tired of trying to repair them—and tired of the thick cardboard stage that was patched and shaky.

He lay very still for a moment and then sat up in bed. He had an idea—a wonderful idea! He couldn't wait to try it. And why wait, anyway? Didn't all those sad broken puppets belong to him?

Quickly he threw back the blankets and jumped out of bed. The marble floor was icy cold but he put on some heavy socks and slippers, then a wool shirt and sweater.

He ran to the cupboard in the kitchen where his father kept a box of tools—a hammer, a saw and nails.

Then he returned to his room. He paused for a moment— to give one last look at the puppet stage and the puppets as he thought of all the times he had used it and the way he made the neighborhood children giggle and laugh so happily.

Then he quickly collected some pieces of wood from the storage room and went to work. First he removed the torn curtains of the stage, thinking as he worked, 'Old and ugly—torn and worn. I won't be needing you anymore!' Next he carefully measured the wood and marked it with a pencil. After he made sure all the measurements were correct, he sawed the pieces of wood into the right sizes. Then it was time to use the hammer and nails. He worked quickly but carefully.

Suddenly his mother put her head inside the door. "Carmello! What is all this hammering? You are making too much noise!"

"I will be finished soon, Mamma—just a few more minutes."

His mother grumbled and closed the door. Carmello went back to work and within ten minutes the stage looked nothing like a stage at all. Quickly he went around the room, gathering the old puppets in his arms. Old and ugly, he thought. Torn and worn, he thought.

He ripped off their little capes full of holes, the shabby skirts and baggy trousers. The hats he threw into the wastepaper basket, but everything else went into the bottom of the old stage. When he had used every scrap of material, he took the faded green curtains and laid them carefully over the torn clothes. Now he had made the stage into a different thing entirely—a perfect bed for a cat and her kittens.

As Carmello sat admiring his work, he heard a cough outside his door and then a knock. "Come in," he called out.

It was Nonno, looking very sick. Walking slowly to Carmello's bed, he said, "I am going to see Doctor Pepolino." He sat down, but when he saw the confusion in the room, he slowly raised his eyes to heaven and, opening the palms of his hands, he said, "Mamma mia! What have you been doing, Carmello? It looks as though a war has just finished here."

Carmello's mother came running in. Her eyes moved quickly around the room, and she also raised her eyes to heaven, stretched out her arms and cried, "Mamma mia, Carmello! What have you done to your puppets?"

Proudly Carmello pointed to his old puppet stage. "I suddenly had an idea," he said. "And I decided to do something about it right away. That is what you always say, Nonno, 'Don't just talk about things—do something about them!' The tabby cat that lives in the courtyard is going to have kittens. I don't want her little family to live through the whole winter out in the cold and rain. If they do, some morning I will probably go out and find the kittens dead—just as I did last winter. Now I have made them a good home from my old stage and they can stay here with me through the winter."

Nonno and Carmello's mother did not look happy. "It is not
a good idea," Nonno said. "We Romans do not like to keep cats
in our houses."

"What can you be thinking of"—shouted Carmello's mother
"to bring a cat and her kittens into our apartment! Your room

is so crowded now there is barely place for your clothes. Never will a cat come into our apartment while I am the Mamma here."

Carmello knew she meant what she said. And knew that his father would agree with her. And even Nonno. It was useless to try to change their ways.

Carmello grabbed a scarf and ran out of the apartment.

In the Piazza Navona the crowds were gathering. From all over Rome, excited groups of children were coming to admire the wonderful toys—and to buy glittering stars, colored lights and candles for their trees.

In the center of the Piazza a strange, ugly little witch came out of her candy house to find out what presents the children wanted for Christmas. It was Befana—the good witch of Christmas, who is so ugly that she is really kind of funny.

"Buon Natale," she croaked in a man's husky voice. "Buon Natale—Merry Christmas!"

But today Befana did not make Carmello laugh, and when a cold spray of water from one of the fountains drenched his sweater, he turned and ran to see the cats.

Quickly he climbed the high wall and jumped into the garden. The cats were huddling under the trees, trying to keep warm. There was the tough gray cat, the sick-looking thin one, the little black lame cat—but where was the tabby?

Every morning Carmello searched the garden and the courtyard, but the tabby had disappeared completely. Then one morning he pulled apart some broken statues that lay in a far part of the garden and gasped, "Ah…"

Three tiny kittens lay curled up near their mother. One was moving its head, trying to nurse, but the others lay still. Carmello touched one of them, prodding it gently with his finger. It moved a little. He touched the other kitten, and it stretched out a feeble paw. Tenderly he pushed the kitten that seemed hungry closer to its mother's breast and then, quickly climbing the garden wall, he leaped down into the Via della Scala.

Carmello ran back to the apartment, where Nonno lay sick in bed, his gnarled old hands busy repairing his puppets.

"Nonno! Nonno!" Carmello shouted as he opened the door.

He sat on the bed and tried to catch his breath. "Nonno, I have found the tabby! And she has had her kittens! There are only three of them and I think two are almost dead—but I am not sure. And Nonno—it is getting so cold outside."

Nonno looked up from his work. "I have been thinking about the tabby," he said. "And I have talked to your mother about her. There is a little sheltered spot on the balcony outside your room. Let's keep the tabby there on the warmer days. When it is very cold you may bring her and the kittens just inside the door to your room but remember—on each warm day, out they go again. Don't forget."

Carmello ran to get the bed, raced down the stairs and leaped over the garden wall. It had begun to rain, and already little streams and rivers were forcing the cats to move to higher ground.

Carmello lifted away the icy stones that protected the tabby's shelter. She raised her head quickly to see what was happening, her eyes large, her ears erect. She allowed Carmello to lift her gently into the bed and quickly afterward, the three little kittens. Then he carefully carried the little house up to the apartment and into his room.

After they were placed next to the balcony door—just as Nonno had instructed—Carmello brought a rug from the hall and lay down on it to watch the kittens groping for their mother's breast. Soon each of the kittens were nursing happily.

Christmas morning dawned bright and cold. It seemed early, but Carmello had slept longer than he realized. Waiting for him near the little green tree in the living room were his family, already dressed and having their coffee.

"Merry Christmas," his mother and father said.

"Merry Christmas, Carmello," said Nonno.

Carmello wished them all a Merry Christmas, but as he spoke, he looked at the presents under the tree and felt a thick lump of sadness forming in his throat. None of the brightly wrapped presents was big enough to be the box of puppets he wanted.

"Well, Carmello—why don't you open your presents?" Nonno asked.

Carmello reached for a bright green box. He took off the ribbon and paper. Inside was a heavy blue sweater. "It is something you badly need," his mother said.

Carmello thanked her and opened another package, tangling the ribbon in his haste.

"Patience," his father said. "Don't be so excited."

But Carmello couldn't help it, and finally the lid was off, the box was open. Inside was a puppet—one of the wonderful wooden puppets with a bright red coat, blue eyes and a devilish smile!

Carmello flung his arms around his parents and kissed them. "I know that you wanted the whole set of wooden puppets," his father said, "but they are very expensive. We can't promise it, but we will try to get you another one for your birthday. Now go on—open your other present."

A fairly small box from Nonno was next. Everyone laughed as Carmello tangled the ribbon again. When it was finally off, he slid back the lid of the box slowly and there was—could it possibly be? A cat? No—but almost like a cat!

It was a cat puppet!

So that was one of the things that had been keeping Nonno so busy these last weeks!

The old man smiled as he watched Carmello rub the soft fur of the puppet against his cheek. "I have never seen a cat puppet before but, why not? A young man like you, Carmello, wants to try new ways."

Carmello hugged and kissed his grandfather. He was just sticking his hand inside the puppet when Nonno said, "I have another present for you, Carmello—but this one you can't un-wrap."

Nonno took Carmello's hand and looked into his eyes. Then he said, "Doctor Pepolino says that I am getting better but I must not spend too many more years working in the park. Now is the time to teach you. You will come with me on Saturdays —and on Sundays, if you like. I'll show you how to work all the puppets—what voices to use—all the little tricks a puppeteer must learn. And then someday—perhaps in two or three years— you will carry on the Pulcinella show in the park. And maybe, when you are an old man, your little grandchildren will run after you and beg, 'Please let me work the puppets, let me go behind the stage.' "

Carmello was too surprised and happy to speak.

So things did happen after all—after you waited and waited and thought they never would. He began to play with his new puppets but then he thought he heard a faint meowing coming from his room and he went to take care of the tabby and her kittens.

ARNOLD DOBRIN

On his first day in Rome, Henry James wrote in his journal: "Now, for the first time, I live." I wish I too could have felt such a sudden poetic revelation but the truth was far different. I was confused by the narrow streets and piazzas, distracted by the noise, made ill by the cooking and maddened by the traffic. On my second trip I explored the city more thoroughly, felt comfortable and stopped complaining. Three years later I went to Rome to live and then, very suddenly, the miracle happened. The layers of history were no longer simply 'significant historical sites' but an integral part of the life around me. I saw that the famous urbane indifference of the Romans is no thicker than a slice of Italian veal. I grew to love the fragrance of the café espresso drifting through the streets in the late afternoon; I wanted my coffee blacker and stronger. And when I began to understand the attitude of the Romans toward their children I realized that now, for the first time, I was really beginning to live...."

Arnold Dobrin was born in Omaha, Nebraska, brought up in Los Angeles and now lives in Westport, Conn., with his wife and two children. He is the author of LITTLE MONK AND THE TIGER, A Tale of Thailand, and TARO AND THE SEA TURTLES, A Tale of Japan.